STAR TREK

cross-stitch

Gallery Books
A Division of Simon & Schuster, Inc.
1230 Avenue of the Americas
New York, NY 10020

First Gallery Books trade paperback edition May 2013

GALLERY BOOKS and colophon are registered trademarks of Simon & Schuster, Inc.

For information about special discounts for bulk purchases, please contact Simon & Schuster Special Sales at 1-866-506-1949 or business@simonandschuster.com.

The Simon & Schuster Speakers Bureau can bring authors to your live event. For more information or to book an event contact the Simon & Schuster Speakers Bureau at 1-866-248-3049 or visit our website at www.simonspeakers.com.

Star Trek Cross-Stitch is produced by becker&mayer!, Bellevue, Washington
www.beckermayer.com

Designer: Megan Sugiyama and Aileen Morrow
Editor: Kjersti Egerdahl
Photo researcher: Kara Stokes
Production coordinator: Tom Miller
Managing editor: Michael del Rosario
Design assistance: Sam Dawson and Bill Whitaker

Manufactured in Korea

10 9 8 7 6 5 4 3 2 1

Library of Congress Cataloging-in-Publication Data is available upon request.

ISBN 978-1-4767-1866-8

CONTENTS

introduction

Sitting around the television to watch episodes of *Star Trek: The Next Generation* was a weekly ritual for my family. *Star Trek* transported me out of my life of school and homework into the exciting new future of spaceships, aliens, and advanced technology. Now, with the ability to stream on demand, many of us are able to go back and revisit the episodes and series of our childhood as well as the series that came before our time.

Crafting and watching television is a perfect combination: relaxing with *Star Trek* while creating a piece of art you can be proud of. You can complete any of these fun, easy projects while re-watching your favorite episodes. Why not do all thirty of them? Decorate your walls, clothe your kids, and keep your place in your favorite book, all with artwork that declares your devotion to *Star Trek*!

Cross-stitch is a great beginners craft because it is easy to learn and the materials are quite cheap. You should be able to complete any of the projects in the book for under twenty dollars, and once you've bought the main materials, you'll be able to complete more projects even more cheaply. You will be able to find all of the supplies you need at your local craft store; or if you don't live near one, you can always order what you need through an online supplier.

MATERIALS

Aida Fabric: Aida is a fabric with regular spacing of threads: it will help you keep all the crosses in your stitching even in size and spacing. The most commonly used aida fabric is fourteen-count, which means that there are 14 stitches per inch.

Thread: The most common thread used in cross-stitch is DMC brand. Each color has a color code, which is used throughout the patterns in this book.

Needle: A tapestry needle is recommended because it is a blunt needle. Size 24 is best for 14-count aida fabric.

Embroidery Hoop: The most common holder for your fabric is an embroidery hoop; it's nice because it gives you a good grip while you are stitching with your other hand.

Waste Canvas: This is a temporary type of aida fabric for stitching onto objects like shirts, pillows, or bags. It's held together with water-soluble glue, so you can wet the canvas and pull out the threads, leaving only your nice, even stitches.

Plastic Canvas: This is a plastic version of aida cloth for making solid or 3-D objects like the Christmas tree ornaments in this book.

getting started

The first thing to do is to cut your aida cloth to a larger size than the pattern (about two inches or more in each direction). You can always trim it when you frame it, but you can't put it back! Next, you need to find the center of the fabric. The easiest way is to fold the cloth vertically, and then horizontally; the center will be where the two folds meet. Once you have the center marked, you can put your fabric into your embroidery hoop.

Embroidery floss is made up of six strands, but that's a little thick for cross-stitching. Cut your first color to a length of about two feet and separate out two of the six strands to use. It's typically best to start with lighter colors and finish with darker colors. The easiest way to start is to simply tie a small knot in the end of your two threads— the only downside to knots is that when you frame your piece, it can add an uneven bulk to the back and prevent it from lying flat. So try to tie a small, tight knot.

Each stitch is an X of thread with each corner of the X placed in a hole in the aida fabric. Make sure that you cross each X in the same direction so that it is consistent throughout the whole piece. To finish a thread, just run it through the back of a few stitches and cut it off. Try to work out from the center as much as possible so as not to cause wrinkles in the fabric.

To finish your piece, you will want to clean and iron it before you put it in a frame. To clean it, use a mild detergent and wash it by hand, laying it out flat to dry. It is best to iron on a low setting, with no water, on the back of the project. After your project is clean and ironed, you can choose the perfect frame and hang it on the wall.

Happy stitching!

Enterprise
Sweet
Enterprise

"You treat her like a lady, and she'll always bring you home."

–Dr. McCoy, "Encounter at Farpoint, Part I"

enterprise sweet enterprise

Pattern by John Lohman • **Stitched by Carrie Musser**

I can imagine this hanging in the quarters of a crew member aboard the *Enterprise* as a play off the classic "Home Sweet Home" cross-stitch of the past. Sitting down to work on a cross-stitch project is a great way to relax and forget about the stresses of daily life—including but not limited to Borg attacks, warp core breaches, or transporter malfunctions that split you into a positive being and an evil twin.

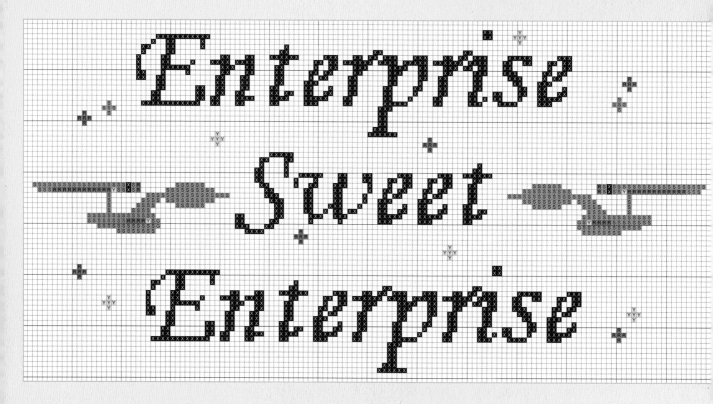

 DMC 606 Burnt Orange-Red    DMC 437 Tan    DMC 310 Black

DMC 318 Steel Grey   DMC 973 Canary

1. Cut your white fabric to a minimum of 5" × 10". I recommend 9"× 11" so it will fit nicely into an 8" × 10" frame. Find and mark the center of the fabric.

2. Starting with the black (310) center, stitch the W in SWEET. Work to the left, and then to the right to finish the word. Count up 13 stitches, and then 1 stitch right from the center to start the bottom corner of the P in the top ENTERPRISE. Finish off the black text by counting down 18 from the center into the R of the bottom ENTERPRISE. Use a new black thread for each word so as not to leave extra black thread on the back of the white fabric.

3. Next, stitch the right *Enterprise* in gray (318), counting 28 to the right and up 1 of the center. Stitch the saucer first and follow the gray to the main body and engines. Start a new gray thread and stitch the left *Enterprise* in the same manner. Finish the gray by stitching the two gray stars and tie each one off.

4. After you finish the gray of the ships, stitch the red (606) and yellow (973) elements that are spread throughout the pattern. I recommend tying off each separate object so that you do not end up with messy threads zigzagging across the back of the fabric.

5. Finish the pattern with the 2 gold (437) stitches at the front of each ship. Optionally, use the gold DMC E3821 metallic thread. You can add a few gold stars to the pattern too.

"In the strict scientific sense, Doctor, we all feed on death . . . even vegetarians."

–Spock, "Wolf in the Fold"

red shirt

Pattern by John Lohman

Stitched by Phillip Coxwell

Starfleet security officers often
had a short acting career—there
always seemed to be one new red
shirt accompanying the officers
on the landing parties. Whether
strangled by Ruk, shot by the
Gorn, or having the corpuscles
of their blood forcibly extracted
by a dikironium cloud, they all
had the honor of shielding more
important characters. Immortalize
all of the many fallen red shirts
in this project.

 R DMC 304 Christmas Red

 P DMC 407 Desert Sand

 X DMC 310 Black

D DMC 902 Garnet

G DMC 3023 Brown-Gray

INSTRUCTIONS

1. Cut your white fabric to a minimum of 4" × 6". I recommend 6" × 8" so it will fit nicely into a 5" × 7" frame. Find and mark the center of the fabric.

2. Count 1 stitch to the left and finish the large red (304) section of the uniform. I recommend working large areas in horizontal lines, doing half stitches all the way to the end of the row, then coming back on the same row to finish each X.

3. Count down 4 and 9 left from the center to stitch the shadow of dark red (902) on the arm. Stitch down and to the right to finish off the shadow.

4. Next, finish the small areas of skin (407) and the gold badge (3023). If you want the badge to stand out more, try using a metallic gold thread (E3821).

5. Lastly, count up 4 and right 1 from the center into the N of EXPENDABLE to do the black (310) text. Work to the right through NDABLE, then start a new thread in the E and stitch the EXPE to the left. If you have thread left, you can jump to the black shadow of the badge and neckline without starting a new thread, because the thread will be hidden behind the red stitches.

THE NEXT GENERATION

"You are trifling with the primal instincts of our species. I must warn you that human parents are quite willing to die for their children."

–Captain Picard, "When the Bough Breaks"

the next generation baby's one-piece

Pattern by John Lohman

Stitched by Amy Lohman

Star Trek: The Next Generation (TNG) was an awesome spin-off of the original episodes, and now you can let your kid be your "next generation" spin-off. Many argue that TNG is better than the original Star Trek—and hopefully your next generation of kids will be better off than you were. Dress up your "Number One" with this Next Generation one-piece.

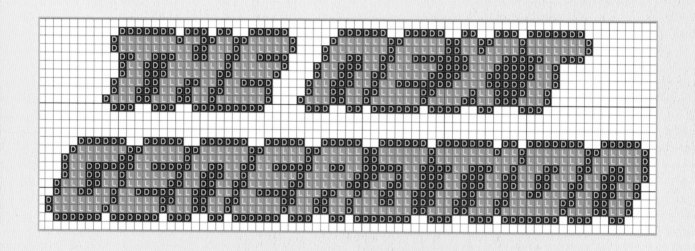

 DMC 996 Electric Blue

 DMC 797 Royal Blue

1. Cut a 3" × 6" rectangle out of your waste aida canvas and stitch it onto the baby's one-piece with a few baste stitches. These will be removed later, but they will keep everything aligned until you are finished cross-stitching. Mark the center of your waste fabric.

2. It is very important that you work your way out from the center, as it will smooth out the one-piece. If you don't work out from the center, you could end up with bunched-up fabric in the middle.

3. Count up 3 and right 1 from the center into the bottom of the N in NEXT and stitch the light blue (996), working to the right to finish the word. Start a new thread in the E of THE and stitch the E, H, and T to the left.

4. Count down 3 from the center into the top of the R and stitch the RATION to the right. Start a new thread and stitch the E, N, E, and G to the left.

5. Finish with the dark blue (797) border around all the letters.

6. Once the stitching is done, remove the baste stitches and wet the waste fabric. Waste fabric is held together by water-soluble glue and will fall apart into individual threads. Use tweezers to remove each waste fabric thread individually.

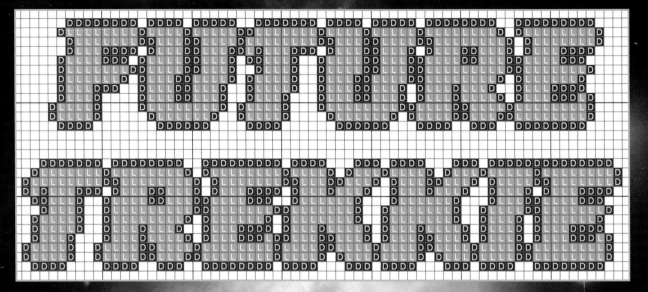

 DMC 996 Electric Blue

 DMC 797 Royal Blue

"Change is the essential process of all existence."

–Spock, "Let That Be Your Last Battlefield"

Future Trekkie

Pattern by John Lohman

Every parent has a strong desire to influence his or her kids to become better people: this begins by introducing them to *Star Trek* at a very young age. Classical music, the alphabet, and reading are all overrated. Your little one may not be able to talk yet, but this one-piece will declare the kid a Trekkie for life.

★ INSTRUCTIONS

1. Cut a 3" × 6" rectangle out of your waste aida canvas and stitch it onto the baby's one-piece with a few baste stitches. These will be removed later, but they will keep everything aligned until you are finished cross-stitching. Mark the center of your waste fabric. It is very important that you work your way out from the center, as it will smooth out the one-piece.

2. Count up 4 and right 1 from the center into the light blue (996) of the second U in FUTURE and stitch your way to the right through the URE. Start a new thread and stitch T, U, and F to the left to finish the top word.

3. Count down 3 from from the center into the first K and stitch KKIE to the right. Start a new thread and stitch the E, R, and T to the right.

4. Finish with the dark blue (797) border around all the letters.

5. Once the stitching is done, remove the baste stitches and wet the waste fabric. Waste fabric is held together by water-soluble glue and will fall apart into individual threads. Use tweezers to remove each waste fabric thread individually.

"Crazy way to travel . . . spreading a man's molecules all over the universe."

–Dr. McCoy, "Obsession"

beam me up, scotty!

Pattern by John Lohman • **Stitched by John Lohman**

Is there anyone left in the Alpha Quadrant who wouldn't recognize this catchphrase? Its only rival in the *Star Trek* world has got to be "To boldly go …" Display the popular catchphrase on your wall for all to see. Watch to see who doesn't get it: they clearly need your help. The borders of this design feature *The Original Series*'s version of the *Enterprise* beaming up crew members from Earth, on the left, and the strange new world of Qo'noS on the right.

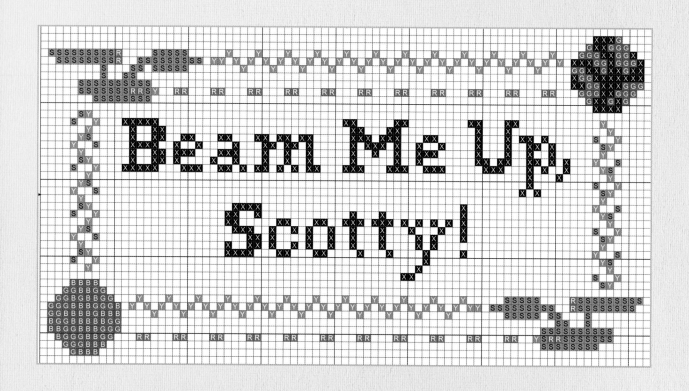

Beam Me Up Scotty!

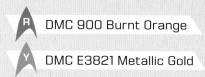
R DMC 900 Burnt Orange

Y DMC E3821 Metallic Gold

B DMC 995 Electric Blue

G DMC 701 Christmas Green

H DMC 310 Black

S DMC 647 Beaver Gray

1. Cut your white fabric to a minimum of 3.1" × 5.9". I recommend 6" × 8" so it will fit nicely into a 5" × 7" frame. Find and mark the center of the fabric.

2. Count up 3 and right 1 from the center into the M in ME and stitch the black (310) of the top line of text: first ME, then UP, and finally BEAM. Tie off your black thread after you complete each word. Count down 3 and right 2 from the center into the first T in SCOTTY and finish the bottom line of text with a new thread, stitching first to the right, and then back to the left.

3. Count up from the center 12 and left 26 to stitch the gray (647) in the upper left *Enterprise*. You will be in the lower right corner of the ship, so finish the main body, and then move to the engines, and finally to the big saucer. Then count down 14 from the center and right 23 to stitch the lower right *Enterprise* using a new gray thread.

4. Count 25 down from the lower left corner of the top *Enterprise* and stitch the blue (995) followed by the green (701) on the planet Earth.

5. Count 51 to the right from the tip of the top *Enterprise* and stitch the black (310) followed by the green (701) of QO'NOS.

6. Connect the four corner objects with the gold (E3821) and gray (647) and finish off the project by stitching the red (900) dashed lines and features on the *Enterprises*.

CHOOSE WISELY OR

"The best diplomat that I know is a fully-loaded phaser bank."

–Scotty, "A Taste of Armageddon"

choose wisely

Pattern by John Lohman • **Stitched by Callie Beck**

Kirk or Picard? *TOS* or *TNG* (or *DS9*, if you want to seem original . . .)? Fans of *Star Trek* TV have been engaged in this difficult debate for years. Do you stick with whichever series was on the air when you were a kid, or is that too easy? This pattern features two hand phasers: one from *Star Trek: The Original Series* and one from *Star Trek: The Next Generation*. So, which will it be? The campy energy of *TOS* or the intellectual questions of *TNG*? Better choose wisely.

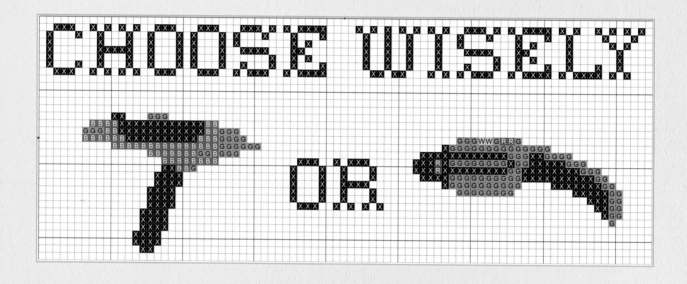

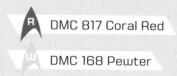

B	DMC 931 Antique Blue	**R** DMC 817 Coral Red	**X** DMC 310 Black
G	DMC 318 Steel Grey	**W** DMC 168 Pewter	

★ INSTRUCTIONS

1. Cut your white fabric to a minimum of 2.4" × 6". I recommend 6" × 8" so it will fit nicely into a 5" × 7" frame. Find and mark the center of the fabric.

2. Count 14 left from the center and finish the gray (318) of the left phaser. Start a new gray thread and count 16 right of the center to do the gray (318) on the right phaser.

3. Count 18 left of the center to stitch the blue (931) of the left phaser; work from the right side of the phaser to the left.

4. Complete the red (817) and white (168) highlights on the right phaser.

5. Lastly, count down 4 into the R in OR and stitch your way through the black (310) areas of the text and phasers. Use a different black thread for each of the words and phasers so that you don't have black thread crisscrossing the back of your project and showing through the white fabric.

"...a dream that became a reality
and spread throughout the stars..."

–Captain Kirk, "Whom Gods Destroy"

federation seal

Pattern by John Lohman • **Stitched by Lindsay Bickford**

The United Federation of Planets was founded on Earth in 2161 by humans, Vulcans, Andorians, and Tellarites, and eventually spread democracy to more than 150 planets throughout the Milky Way Galaxy. Salute this Federation flag as a symbol of your devotion to the *Star Trek* ideal of a more unified and peaceful society. Or carry the message with you: try this pattern on the flap of a black messenger bag.

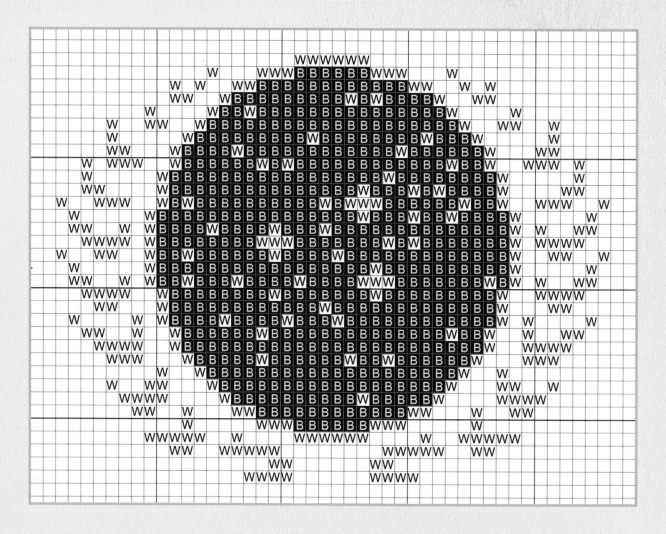

 **B** DMC 796 Royal Blue   **W** DMC 5200 Snow White

1. Cut your black fabric to a minimum of 3.4" X 2.6". I recommend 6" X 8" so it will fit nicely into a 5" X 7" frame. Find and mark the center of the fabric.

2. Starting with white (5200), from the center, count 1 stitch up and 1 stitch to the right. Complete the stars that make up the center of the logo; then complete the outside edge of the blue circle

3. Lastly, from the center, complete the blue (796) circle. It is best to work out from the center as much as possible so as not to cause wrinkles in the fabric.

"Captain's log, Stardate 9522.6: I've never trusted Klingons, and I never will."

–Captain Kirk, *Star Trek VI: The Undiscovered Country*

Captains of Star Trek hand towel

Pattern by John Lohman

Stitched by China Darley

It is hard to imagine the different *Star Trek* series without the leadership of each of the respective captains. Almost every debate about which series was best ends up degrading into a debate about which captain was best: Kirk, with his physical prowess and lady-killer ways; Picard, with his calm and calculating intelligence; Sisko, as a parent and skilled shouter; Janeway, as the strong, isolated female captain; or Archer, with his flexible morals. Which captain was your favorite?

H DMC 3781 Dark Mocha Brown	**W** DMC 5200 Snow White	**N** DMC 3860 Cocoa
O DMC 829 Golden Olive	**F** DMC 844 Beaver Gray	**L** DMC 307 Lemon
S DMC 676 Light Old Brown	**R** DMC 304 Christmas Red	**A** DMC 445 Lemon
G DMC 680 Dark Old Gold	**B** DMC 797 Royal Blue	**M** DMC 434 Brown
Y DMC 728 Golden Yellow	**H** DMC 310 Black	**P** DMC 754 Peach
D DMC 898 Coffee Brown	**E** DMC 415 Pearl Gray	**K** DMC 781 Topaz
T DMC 3782 Light Mocha Brown		

1. Find a dish towel or bath towel that has a strip of aida cloth along the bottom edge. These can be found online or in any major craft or fabric store. The aida cloth portion of the towel will need to be at least 2.1" × 3.9" to fit the design. Find and mark the center of the aida section.

2. Start with the light skin tone (676) across the faces followed by Sisko's brown (434) skin tone. Start a new brown thread (434) to complete Archer's hair. Start a new thread for each face to avoid leaving too much extra thread on the back of the design.

3. Starting a new thread for each uniform, stitch the yellows (728 and 307), red (304), and blue (797) of each captain followed by the black (310) of each uniform.

4. Finish off the remaining isolated details of the eyes, hands, hair, and face.

"Five-card stud, nothing wild . . .
and the sky's the limit."

–Captain Picard, "All Good Things . . ."

Star trek communicator badge on messenger bag

Pattern by John Lohman

Stitched by John Lohman

As you walk around a *Star Trek* convention or a newly discovered planet, you'll need something to carry all of your essentials. You can't leave home without your *TNG* DVDs, Starfleet uniform, phaser, tricorder, and communicator— and they certainly don't carry themselves! Take your favorite bag and make it even better by emblazoning it with this iconic *Star Trek* symbol.

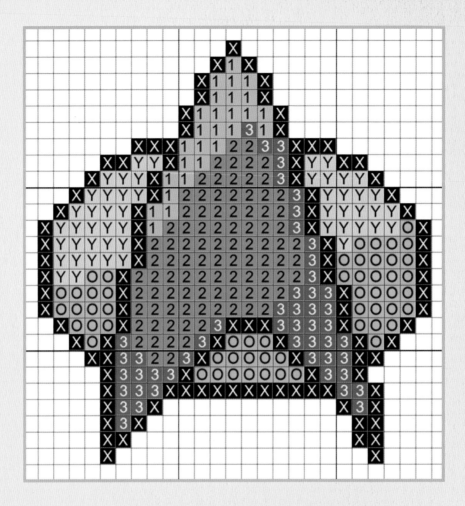

 DMC 647 Medium Beaver Gray

 DMC 741 Tangerine

 DMC 310 Black

 DMC 648 Light Beaver Gray

DMC 676 Old Gold

DMC 646 Dark Beaver Gray

★ INSTRUCTIONS

1. Find a messenger bag that needs a makeover or do a quick Internet search for a one-piece messenger bag pattern and sew your own.

2. Cut a 3" × 3" square out of your waste aida canvas and stitch it onto your messenger bag with a few baste stitches. These will be removed later, but they will keep everything aligned until you are finished cross-stitching. Mark the center of your waste fabric.

3. It is very important that you work your way out from the center, as it will smooth out the fabric. If you don't work out from the center, you could end up with bunched-up fabric in the middle.

4. Start in the center by stitching the medium gray (647) center of the badge. Next, stitch the light gray (648) above and the dark gray below (646).

5. Next, fill in the light yellow (676) around the outside of the gray followed by the darker yellow (741) right below it.

6. Lastly, stitch the black (310) border around the outside of the communication badge.

7. Once the stitching is done, remove the baste stitches and wet the waste fabric. Waste fabric is held together by water-soluble glue and will fall apart into individual threads. Use tweezers to remove each waste fabric thread individually.

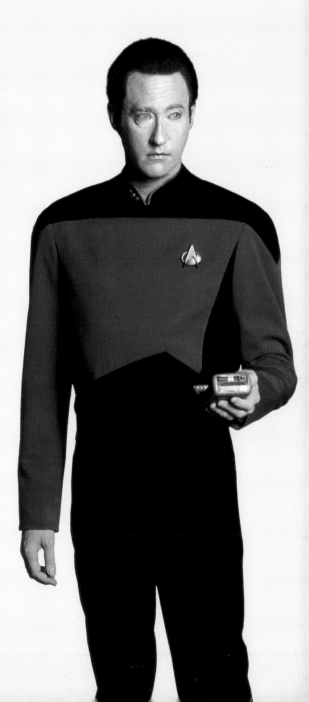

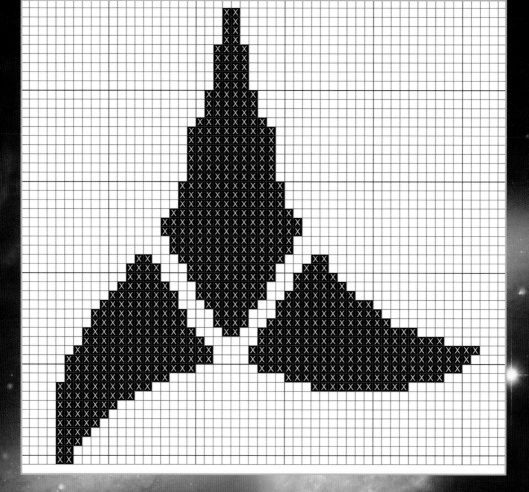

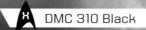 DMC 310 Black

"Revenge is a dish best served cold."

–Klingon proverb, *Star Trek II: The Wrath of Khan*

kLingon Logo on messenger bag

Pattern by John Lohman

This pattern would look great on a light-colored messenger bag. Drivers will certainly think twice about encroaching on your bike lane. You could also strap a *bat'leth* to the back of your bag, but law enforcement might frown on that.

instructions

1. Get out your biking bag or do a quick Internet search for a one-piece messenger bag pattern and sew your own.

2. Cut a 4.5" × 5" rectangle out of your waste aida canvas and stitch it onto your messenger bag with a few baste stitches. These will be removed later, but they will keep everything aligned until you are finished cross-stitching. Mark the center of your waste fabric. It is very important that you work your way out from the center, as it will smooth out the fabric.

3. Start stitching the black (310) in the center and work your way up to the point. Start a new thread and stitch the bottom part of the center spire. Stitch the other two spires, working from the parts closest to the center of the cloth to the outer edges.

4. Once the stitching is done, remove the baste stitches and wet the waste fabric. Waste fabric is held together by water-soluble glue and will fall apart into individual threads. Use tweezers to remove each waste fabric thread individually.

"By golly, Jim . . . I'm beginning to
think I can cure a rainy day."

–Dr. McCoy, "The Devil in the Dark"

he's dead, jim . . .

Pattern by John Lohman • **Stitched by Callie Beck**

Dr. McCoy said this line (or variations close to it) twenty times throughout the
original *Star Trek*. The life of an *Enterprise* crew member can often be cut short;
this is especially true for the many red shirts that have died under McCoy's
watch. My personal favorite death scene is when Yeoman Leslie Thompson
is killed by the Kelvans in "By Any Other Name": they transform her into a
dehydrated crystalline block and crush her. She also had the distinction of being
the only female red shirt to die in the original series.

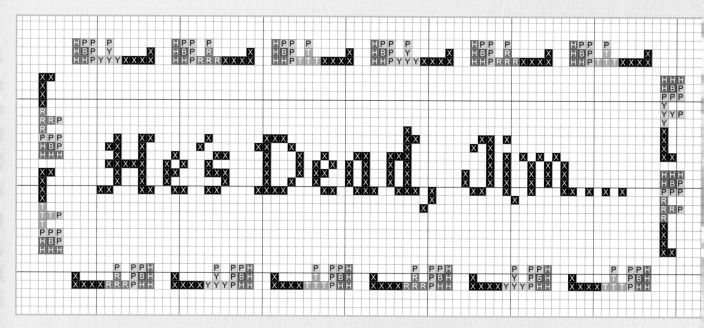

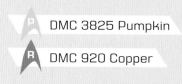

B — DMC 995 Dark Electric Blue

T — DMC 996 Medium Electric Blue

H — DMC 780 Topaz

P — DMC 3825 Pumpkin

R — DMC 920 Copper

X — DMC 310 Black

Y — DMC 3821 Straw

1. Cut your white fabric to a minimum of 2.5" × 6". I recommend 6" × 8" so it will fit nicely into a 5" × 7" frame. Find and mark the center of the fabric.

2. Starting with black (310), count up 1 and start the text with the A in DEAD. Stitch right and left of the center to finish off the text, then work in a circle to stitch the legs of each of the people. You can continue the same thread for all the black stitches.

3. Counting down 12 and left 1 from the center, stitch the brown (780) hair of each person, followed by the skin (3825) of each face and hand, and then the blue (995) of each eye. Work from the bottom center around in a circle.

4. Lastly, stitch the red (920), gold (3821), and blue (996) of each uniform.

"This child is about to wipe out every living thing on Earth. Now, what do you suggest we do . . . spank it?"

–Dr. McCoy, *Star Trek: The Motion Picture*

tng communicator badge on bib

Pattern by China Darley

Stitched by China Darley

Most parents like to make silly noises when they feed their young kids: whooshing airplanes, beeping trucks, motorboats—anything to get them to take a bite. However, with this bib on, you'll have to change it up with some pew-pewing phasers, blamming photon torpedoes, and whooshing starships going to warp speed. This communication badge would also look great on a baby's one-piece.

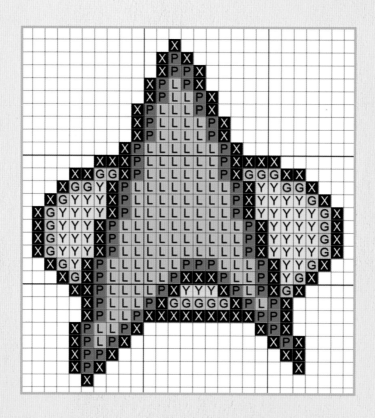

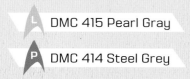
DMC 415 Pearl Gray

DMC 972 Canary

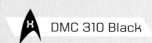
DMC 310 Black

DMC 414 Steel Grey

DMC 743 Yellow

instructions

1. Find a simple, solid-colored baby's bib (or a onesie, if you prefer).

2. Cut a 3" ✕ 3" square out of your waste aida canvas and stitch it onto your bib with a few baste stitches. These will be removed later, but they will keep everything aligned until you are finished cross-stitching. Mark the center of your waste fabric.

3. It is very important that you work your way out from the center, as it will smooth out the bib. If you don't work out from the center, you could end up with bunched-up fabric in the middle.

4. Start in the center by stitching the light gray (415), working up to the top, and then back down to the lower corners. Outline the light part with the dark gray (414) around the edges.

5. Next, stitch the light yellow (743) portions on either side of the gray badge. Outline the light yellow with dark yellow (972).

6. Finally, stitch the outer black (310) border around the communication badge.

7. Once the stitching is done, remove the baste stitches and wet the waste fabric. Waste fabric is held together by water-soluble glue and will fall apart into individual threads. Use tweezers to remove each waste fabric thread individually.

TROUBLE?

"Its trilling seems to have a tranquilizing effect on the human nervous system. Fortunately, of course . . . I am immune to its effect."

–Spock, "The Trouble with Tribbles"

trouble? (with tribbles)

Pattern by John Lohman • **Stitched by Megan N. O'Donnell**

"The Trouble with Tribbles" is one of the most iconic episodes of *The Original Series*. The cute little fur balls won their way into the crew's hearts, even the ever-logical Spock's. Not only were they cute, but they saved an entire planet from eating poisoned grain while identifying a Klingon saboteur! Hang this hoop and cross-stitch on the wall, where "they'll be no tribble at all."

5	DMC 842 Light Beige Brown	
7	DMC 3863 Mocha Beige	
8	DMC 840 Medium Beige Brown	
1	DMC 168 Very Light Pewter	
4	DMC 317 Pewter Gray	
3	DMC 169 Light Pewter	
X	DMC 310 Black	
2	DMC 318 Steel Gray	
6	DMC 437 Tan	

1. Cut your white fabric to a minimum of 2.2" × 2.9" . I recommend 6" × 6" so it will fit nicely into a 5" embroidery hoop. Pick the size of your embroidery hoop before you cut your fabric. Find and mark the center of the fabric.

2. Count up 1 from the center and start stitching with the light brown (842). The lightest brown is mostly at the top of the tribble, so work your way down through the tribble, switching to each progressively darker color: 437, 3863, and 840.

3. Stitch the two gray tribbles in the same fashion as the brown tribble: from lightest to darkest and from top to bottom: 168, 318, 169, 317.

4. After you finish the three tribbles, count up 9 from the center into the U in TROUBLE. Stitch the black (310) letters to the right first through UBLE? and tie off your thread. Start a new thread and stitch to the left from the center through the O, R, and T to finish.

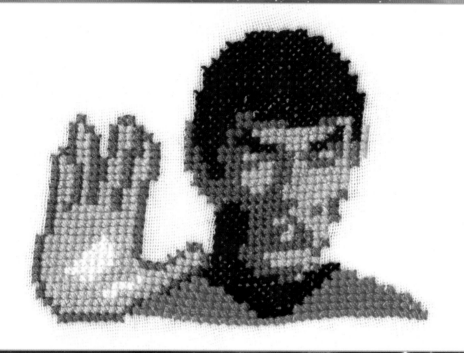

"Logic is the beginning of wisdom; not the end."

–Spock, *Star Trek VI: The Undiscovered Country*

spock baby's one-piece

Pattern by John Lohman

Stitched by Katie Dunn

Logic was the centerpiece of Spock's being and attitude—not so much for two-year-olds. Maybe if you make this shirt for your little ones, some of the logic of Spock's teachings will wear off on them (probably not). If you can't reason with your kids using logic, you can at least teach them how to do the Vulcan salute.

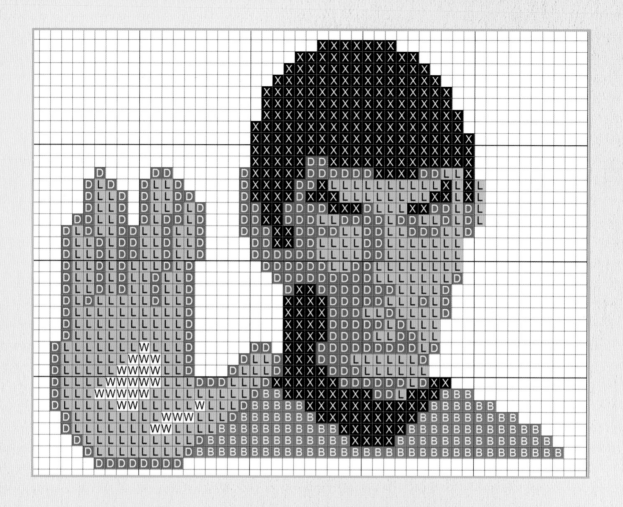

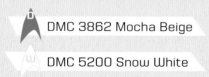 DMC 3862 Mocha Beige

 DMC 738 Tan

 DMC 310 Black

DMC 5200 Snow White

DMC 3843 Electric Blue

1. Cut a 4" X 5" rectangle out of your waste aida canvas and stitch it onto the baby's one-piece with a few baste stitches. These will be removed later, but they will keep everything aligned until you are finished cross-stitching. Mark the center of your waste fabric.

2. It is very important that you work your way out from the center, as it will smooth out the one-piece. If you don't work out from the center, you could end up with bunched-up fabric in the middle.

3. Count 2 to the right from the center and start stitching the light brown (738) of Spock's face. Stitch up and to the right and then around to the bottom of his face. Count over to the top of his thumb and stitch across and up to finish the light brown of his hand.

4. Fill in the two small holes in Spock's hand with white (5200) stitching.

5. Starting at the center, stitch the dark brown (3862) shading of the face. Start a new thread and stitch the dark brown border around the hand.

6. Starting with the sideburn up 1 and left 1 from the center, stitch the black (310) up into the hair; finish with the eyebrows. Start a new thread and count 3 down from the center to stitch the black shadow of the neckline.

7. Finish with the light blue (3843) of Spock's shirt.

8. Once the stitching is done, remove the baste stitches and wet the waste fabric. Waste fabric is held together by water-soluble glue and will fall apart into individual threads. Use tweezers to remove each waste fabric thread individually.

"Everybody remember where we parked."

"They like you very much. But they are not the hell your whales."

–Spock, *Star Trek IV: The Voyage Home*

"everybody remember where we parked."

Pattern by John Lohman   •   Stitched by Camilla Schæffer

This quote is from one of the most memorable scenes in *Star Trek IV*, when Captain Kirk lands the stolen Klingon *bird-of-prey* in Golden Gate Park, San Francisco. The ship is cloaked so as not to arouse a reaction from the residents of Earth in the "latter half of the twentieth century." I spent a large portion of my life living in and around San Francisco, and I am still disappointed that I never walked into an invisible Klingon spaceship.

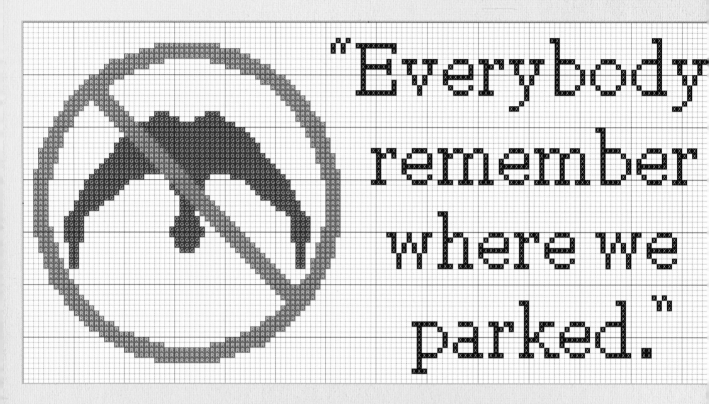

"Everybody remember where we parked."

R · DMC 900 Burnt Orange   G · DMC 645 Beaver Gray   X · DMC 310 Black

1. Cut your white aida fabric to a minimum area of 4.9" × 9.8". I recommend 9" × 11" so it will fit nicely into an 8" × 10" frame. Find and mark the center of the fabric.

2. Count up 4 and right 1 from the center into the first R in REMEMBER and start stitching the black (310) of the text. As you start each line, tie off and start a new thread so as not to leave too much black thread running across the back of the white fabric (it will show through).

3. Count 6 to the left from center to stitch the red (900) of the circle. Work your way around the circle, stitching each horizontal line before dropping down to the next. After the circle is done, stitch the backslash across the center of the circle.

4. Starting at the lower right tip of the Klingon ship, stitch the green-gray (645).

"Dress uniforms—spit and polish. I don't know how much longer I'm gonna be able to stand this. I feel like my neck's in a sling."

–Dr. McCoy, "Journey to Babel"

STAR TREK badge pillows

Pattern by John Lohman

Stitched by John Lohman

The iconic uniforms from *The Original Series* can now be a part of your home in pillow form. *TOS* just wouldn't have been the same without the late-'60s uniforms of velour tunics, short skirts, and black boots. If your significant other doesn't think that *Star Trek* pillows match the current décor of your house, you might have to settle for stitching these on a plain gold, red, or blue shirt.

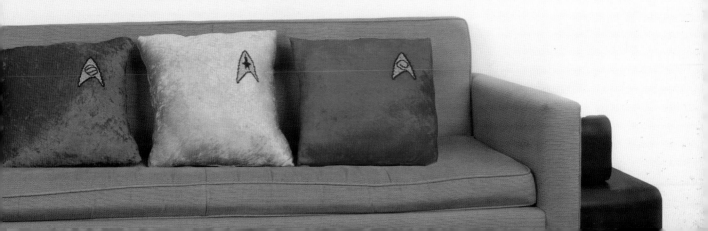

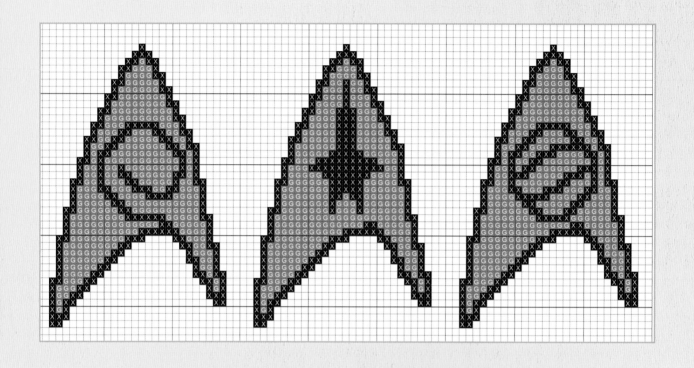

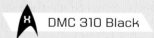 DMC E3821 Light Gold (Metallic)   DMC 310 Black

INSTRUCTIONS

1. Gather your materials: You will need a half yard of each color of fabric and about 32 ounces of stuffing to fill all three pillows. Crushed velour fabric is ideal, but you can use any type of fabric as long as you get the right red, gold, and blue colors of the TOS uniforms.

2. Cut the fabric into two 17" X 17" squares. You want to end up with a 16" square after leaving a ½" seam allowance on each side of the square. I recommend stitching the badge onto the fabric before you sew the two pieces of the pillow together.

3. Cut a 30" X 45" stitch rectangle out of your waste aida canvas and stitch it onto the upper right corner of the pillow fabric with a few baste stitches. These will be removed later, but they will keep everything aligned until you are finished cross-stitching. Mark the center of your waste fabric.

4. Start with the gold metallic (E3821) thread in the center of the waste canvas and stitch out from the center. It is very important that you work your way out from the center, as it will smooth out the pillow fabric. If you don't work out from the center, you could end up with bunched-up fabric in the middle.

5. Fill in the black (310) in the center of the badge and around the outer border.

6. Once the stitching is done, remove the baste stitches and wet the waste fabric. Waste fabric is held together by water-soluble glue and will fall apart into individual threads. Use tweezers to remove each waste fabric thread individually.

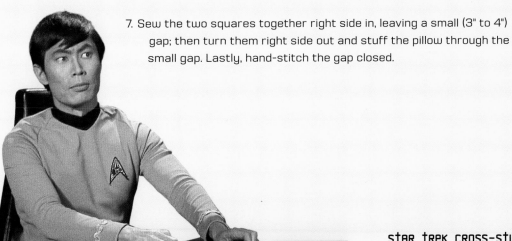

7. Sew the two squares together right side in, leaving a small (3" to 4") gap; then turn them right side out and stuff the pillow through the small gap. Lastly, hand-stitch the gap closed.

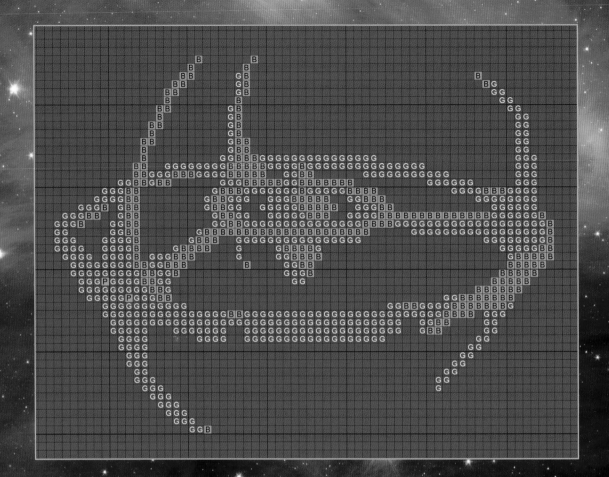

"There's an old saying, fortune favors the bold. Well, I guess we're about to find out."

–Sisko, "Sacrifice of Angels"

deep space 9 pillow

Pattern by John Lohman

Star Trek: Deep Space Nine (*DS9*) might be one of the lesser-known series, but the people who like it *really* like it. This pattern is designed for a dark background.

 INSTRUCTIONS

1. Gather your materials: You will need a half yard of fabric and about 16 ounces of stuffing to fill the pillow. Cut the fabric into two 17" squares. This will make a 16" square pillow after a ½" seam allowance.

2. Cut a 5" × 6" rectangle out of your waste aida canvas and stitch it onto your pillow fabric with a few baste stitches. These will be removed later, but they will keep everything aligned. Mark the center of your waste fabric. It is very important that you work your way out from the center, as it will smooth out the pillow fabric.

3. Start from the center with the gray (317) and stitch around the center part of the *DS9* space station. After the center is finished, work around the outside of the space station.

4. Next, fill in the light blue (3755), starting with the inside and working to the outside of the ship. Add the last two pink (452) lights on the left side of the pattern.

5. Once the stitching is done, remove the baste stitches and wet the waste fabric. Waste fabric is held together by water-soluble glue and will fall apart into individual threads. Use tweezers to remove the threads.

6. Sew the two squares together right side in, leaving a small (3" to 4") gap; then turn them right side out and stuff the pillow through the small gap. Lastly, hand-stitch the gap closed.

I like my coffee
how I like my men:

KLINGON

"I was hoping the Klingons would invade . . . at least they know how to make coffee, even if they are foul-smelling barbarians."

–Arne Darvin, "Trials and Tribble-ations"

Klingon Raktajino

Pattern by Rosier Cade • **Stitched by Rosier Cade**

Raktajino, a type of Klingon coffee, was the beverage of choice for crew members aboard Deep Space 9. Commander Sisko took his with jacarine peel. This pattern also features a modern coffee mug from Quark's Bar on DS9. The mug is also often seen on DS9 in a purple color—if you prefer purple, you can substitute DMC 327 and DMC 552 for the green.

I like my coffee how I like my men:

KLINGON

 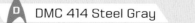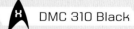

1. Cut your white fabric to a minimum of 4.5" × 4.7". I recommend 6" × 8" so it will fit nicely into a 5" × 7" frame. Find and mark the center of the fabric.

2. Starting from the center, count 2 stitches down and stitch the light green (320) of the coffee cup from top to bottom.

3. One stitch down from the center, finish off the coffee cup with the dark green (367) around the outside border.

4. One stitch up from the center, complete the light gray (415) of the steam, followed by the dark gray (414).

5. Complete the black (310) text by counting 16 stitches up from the center into the E in LIKE. Stitch the E and then the text to the right in MY MEN:. Start a new thread and stitch from the K over to the left to finish the second row of text. Count 5 up and 1 left from the top of the O in HOW; then, with a new thread of black, stitch the top line of text from left to right. Lastly, count 22 down and 1 left from the center into the N in KLINGON and finish the last word.

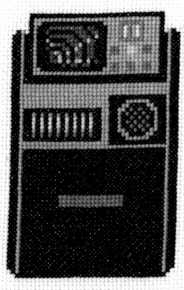

There seems to be no sign of intelligent life anywhere...

"there seems to be no sign of intelligent life anywhere"

Pattern by John Lohman

Stitched by Carolyn Andolina

Though this exact phrase was never uttered in a *Star Trek* episode, similar variations occurred so many times (including unofficial bumper stickers and the like) that it has become a catchphrase in its own right. Oddly enough, it seems like there was almost always intelligent life wherever they went. This design also features the classic science tricorder that was able to scan new worlds, diagnose diseases, analyze technical data, and record observations. This would make a great gift for a friend or family member who isn't a hard-core *Star Trek* fan—yet!

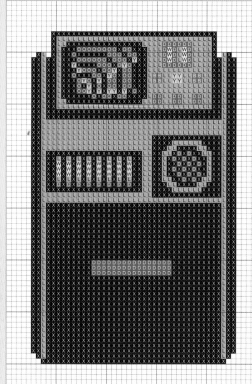

There seems to be no sign of intelligent life anywhere...

D DMC 646 Dark Beaver Gray	**O** DMC 301 Mahogany	**X** DMC 310 Black
L DMC 648 Light Beaver Grey	**W** DMC 5200 Snow White	**Y** DMC 307 Lemon
B DMC 3843 Electric Blue		

1. Cut your white aida fabric to a minimum area of 5.4" × 10". I recommend 9" × 11" so it will fit nicely into an 8" × 10" frame. Find and mark the center of the fabric.

2. Count 4 up from the center into the bottom of the E in BE and start stitching the black (310) letters. I recommend doing one word at a time, tying off, and starting a new thread on the next word. The separation between words is just big enough that you run the risk of the black thread showing through the white fabric.

3. Count 24 to the left from the center and stitch the black (310) of the science tricorder. I recommend working large areas in horizontal lines, doing half stitches all the way to the end of the row, then coming back on the same row to finish each X.

4. After the black is finished, fill in the rest of the tricorder with the light gray (646) and dark gray (648) areas.

5. Finish off the project by stitching the yellow (307), orange (301), blue (3843), and white (5200) highlights.

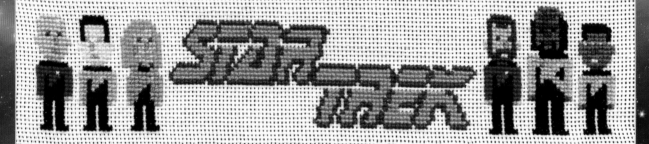

"Our neural pathways have become accustomed to your sensory input patterns."

–Data's definition of friendship, "Time's Arrow, Part I"

the next generation characters hand towel

Pattern by John Lohman

Stitched by Alexandra Pilling

You could fill your bathroom with flowery towels or boring monogrammed towels, but these don't tell people about who you are as a person. Imagine how impressed your houseguests will be when they go to dry their hands and see the cast of *TNG* staring back at them! This towel could also work well in the kitchen, but the idea of spaghetti sauce staining it makes me cringe a little bit.

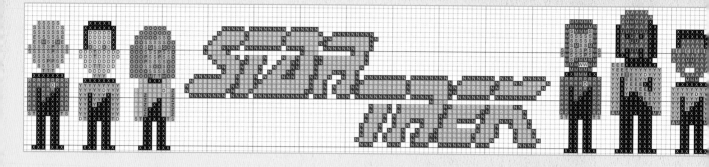

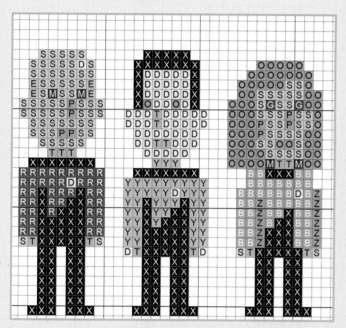

Z DMC 809 Delft Blue	**G** DMC 991 Aquamarine	**D** DMC 445 Lemon	**S** DMC 676 Old Gold
B DMC 996 Electric Blue	**R** DMC 304 Christmas Red	**H** DMC 310 Black	**P** DMC 754 Peach
N DMC 797 Royal Blue	**Y** DMC 166 Moss Green	**A** DMC 434 Brown	**O** DMC 970 Pumpkin
U DMC 3021 Brown Gray	**M** DMC 300 Mahogany	**E** DMC 415 Pearl Gray	
T DMC 3782 Mocha Brown	**W** DMC 5200 Snow White		

★ INSTRUCTIONS

1. Find a hand towel or bath towel that has a strip of aida cloth along the bottom edge. These can be found online or in any major craft or fabric store. The aida cloth portion of the towel will need to be at least 2.3" × 10.7" to fit the design. Find and mark the center of the aida section.

2. Count down 1 from the center and stitch the light blue (996) of the center letters. Stitch the TREK to the right; then start a new thread and stitch the R, A, T, and S to the left. Outline the letters in dark blue (797).

3. For the people, start with the large light-colored areas of skin tone (445 and 676).

4. Stitch the red (304), blue (996), and yellow (166) shirts next, followed by the dark skin tones (434).

5. After that, stitch the light-colored hair colors of orange (970) and brown (300). Finish off the large areas of the characters by stitching the black (310) of the hair and uniforms.

6. Lastly, stitch the small highlights throughout the pattern in seven different colors: 415, 754, 809, 991, 3021, 3782, and 5200.

STAR TREK

Y	DMC 728 Golden Yellow
S	DMC 676 Light Old Gold
L	DMC 372 Light Mustard
M	DMC 3863 Mocha Beige
T	DMC 3782 Mocha Brown
G	DMC 680 Dark Old Gold
W	DMC 5200 Snow White
R	DMC 666 Christmas Red
D	DMC 995 Electric Blue
C	DMC 498 Dark Christmas Red
B	DMC 996 Medium Electric Blue
O	DMC 829 Golden Olive
P	DMC 3811 Turquoise
K	DMC 781 Topaz
X	DMC 310 Black
A	DMC 445 Light Lemon

the original series characters hand towel

Pattern by John Lohman

The main characters of the original *Star Trek* have become so iconic at this point that it's hard to imagine the show being successful if they had cast it differently. The show would have been so different if Christopher Pike had stayed on as the captain. This towel features the icons of *TOS* in a pixelated "Trexels" style.

★ INSTRUCTIONS

1. Find a hand towel or bath towel that has a strip of aida cloth along the bottom edge. These can be found online or in any major craft or fabric store. The aida cloth portion of the towel will need to be at least 2.1" × 9.9" to fit the design. Find and mark the center of the aida section.

2. Count 4 to the right from the center into the T in TREK and stitch the yellow (728) to the right to finish the word. Start a new thread and count 4 to the left of the center into the R and stitch the R, A, T, and S to the right.

3. Next, stitch the gold (680 and 781), blue (996 and 995), and red (666 and 498) tones of each uniform. Make sure to start a new thread for each uniform to keep the back looking neat.

4. Stitch the light skin tone (676) followed by the shading (372), tying off as you finish each character. Then stitch Uhura's skin tone (3863) and shading (829).

5. Stitch the black (310) of the uniforms and the hair. Start a new black thread for each character. Then, add the small finishing stitches: badges, armbands, and facial features in various colors.

ONCE YOU HAVE
THEIR MONEY
YOU NEVER
GIVE IT BACK

"All I ask is a tall ship . . . and a load
of contraband to fill her with."

–Quark, "Little Green Men"

Ferengi Rule of Acquisition #1

Pattern by Lord Libidan

Stitched by Lindsay Bickford

The Ferengi culture is based on the ideal of free enterprise. The Ferengi take the making of money much more seriously than most "hew-mons," and use the Rules of Acquisition to teach young Ferengi how to live a profitable life. Rule #1 is featured in this project, but feel free to pick your own favorite. Some suggestions:

#7: Keep your ears open.

#14: Anything stolen is pure profit.

#18: A Ferengi without profit is no Ferengi at all.

#31: Never insult a Ferengi's mother . . . insult something he cares about instead.

ONCE YOU HAVE
THEIR MONEY
YOU NEVER
GIVE IT BACK

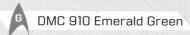 DMC 910 Emerald Green

 DMC 310 Black

1. Cut your white fabric to a minimum of 3.6" × 3.6". I recommend 6" × 8" so it will fit nicely into a 5" × 7" frame. Find and mark the center of the fabric.

2. Starting from the center, count up 1 and right 1 and stitch the green (910) of the Ferengi symbol. Work your way out from the center circle to the edges.

3. Complete the black (310) text by counting 14 stitches up and 2 to the right from the center into the M in MONEY. Work in a counterclockwise circle to finish the text at the top; the words and letters are so close together that you don't need to change threads. For the text at the bottom, start a new thread, count 14 down from the center into the N in NEVER, and work in a clockwise circle.

HOME SWEET HOME

"Only *Qo'noS* endures."

–Klingon death chant, "Tears of the Prophets"

QO'NOS SWEET QO'NOS

Pattern by John Lohman

Stitched by Rosier Cade

Qo'noS (pronounced Kronos) is the home planet of the Klingons and the capital of the Klingon Empire. The Klingons feel as strongly about their home as humans do, so it only makes sense that they would devote cross-stitch pieces to their home world. It must be lonely for Klingons aboard the *Enterprise*; this piece might help them remember the society they've left behind.

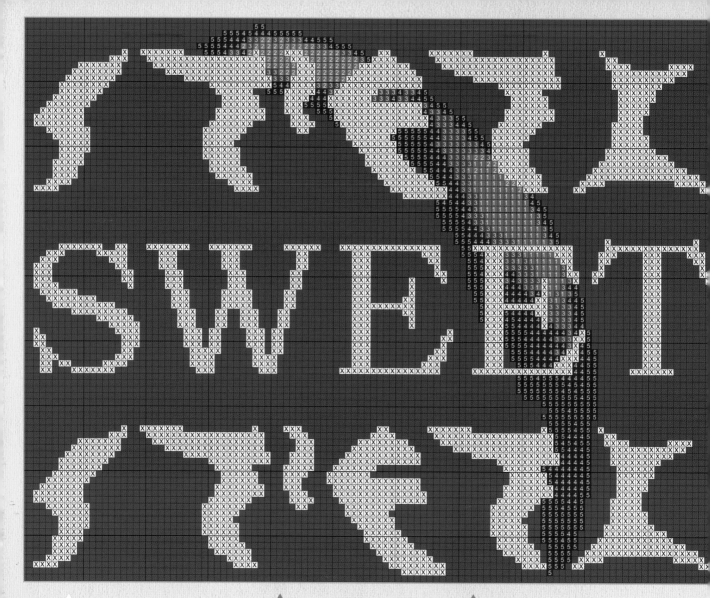

 DMC 5200 Snow White

 DMC 502 Blue Green

5 DMC 890 Pistachio Green

 DMC 3768 Gray Green

3 DMC 501 Dark Blue Green

4 DMC 500 Very Dark Blue Green

★ INSTRUCTIONS

1. Cut your black aida fabric to a minimum area of 6.2" × 7.9". I recommend 9" × 11" so it will fit nicely into an 8" × 10" frame. Find and mark the center of the fabric.

2. Start in the center with white (5200) by stitching to the right through the letters EET and tying off at the bottom of the T. Count 11 down from the bottom of the T and stitch the bottom QO'NOS from right to left, tying off when you reach the left side. Count back up and start a new thread to finish the SW in the middle. After tying off the SW, count up and finish the top QO'NOS.

3. Above the second E, stitch the lightest green (3768) color of the planet. Stitch your way out from the light green center by stitching the outer rings that get progressively darker. Use the pattern numbers 1–5 as a guide for the order to stitch the green shades: 3768, 502, 501, 500, and 890.

"Let's make sure that history never forgets the name . . . *Enterprise*."

–Captain Picard, "Yesterday's *Enterprise*"

I [badge] STAR TREK bookmark

Pattern by John Lohman • Stitched by Deborah Dodson

One of the best *Star Trek* books I've ever read is *First Frontier*. A race of alien reptiles decides to travel back in time and stop the asteroid that caused the extinction of the dinosaurs from hitting Earth. It doesn't get much better than dinosaurs and starships. With hundreds of *Star Trek* novels out there, you'll probably need a bookmark to keep your place.

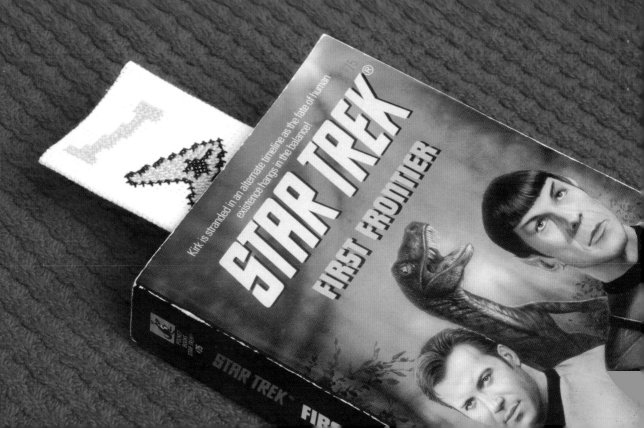

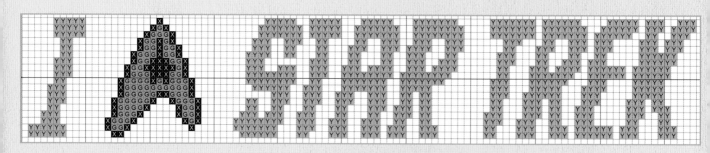

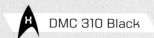

Y DMC 3820 Straw   **G** DMC 3023 Brown-Gray   **X** DMC 310 Black

1. This pattern will make a bookmark that is 7.6" × 1.4". I like to cut my fabric to three times the final width so that I can fold it over the back (trifold) and cover the messy-looking back stitches of the pattern. Cut the fabric to about 8.5" × 4.2" and stitch your design in the center.

2. Start from the center and stitch the yellow (3820) of the A. Stitching one letter at a time, work your way to the right. Make sure to start a new thread when you start on the T in TREK. After you finish TREK, start a new thread and stitch the T and S. Start a new thread and finish the yellow by stitching the I on the far left.

3. Count 28 to the left of the center, in between I and S, and stitch the gray (3023) of the badge. Finish off by doing the black (310) around the border of the badge. Alternately, you can substitute metallic gold (E3821) for the 3023.

4. Trifold the fabric to hide the back of your stitches, and use a white thread to put five evenly spaced stitches across the back. This will ensure that it won't unfold later.

"We are the Borg. Lower your shields and surrender your ships."

–The Borg, Star Trek: First Contact

resistance is futile
bookmark

Pattern by John Lohman and Lord Libidan • Stitched by Jennifer Woodings

I haven't met a Trekkie who doesn't like to read science fiction . . . and I hope I never do. You'll need more than one *Star Trek* bookmark to keep your place as you read through the sci-fi classics. The Borg are definitely one of my favorite enemies of the Federation. This bookmark will help you remember when you are deep in the middle of a good book and trying to go to sleep that "Resistance is futile."

P   DMC 367 Pistachio Green

1   DMC 414 Steel Grey

1   DMC 413 Dark Pewter Gray

2   DMC 317 Pewter Gray

G   DMC 701 Christmas Green

X   DMC 310 Black

1. This pattern will make a bookmark that is 5.6" ✕ 2.1". I like to cut my fabric to three times the final width so that I can fold it over the back (trifold) and cover the messy-looking back stitches of the pattern. Cut the bookmark to about 7" ✕ 6.1" and stitch your design in the center.

2. Count up 2 from the center into the E in RES to stitch the black (310) text. Finish the RE, and then work your way to the right through RESISTANCE. Count down 5 from RESISTANCE and start a new thread for the second line of text.

3. Count up 3 from the text for the top border and down 3 for the bottom border and stitch the light green (367). Count your stitches carefully based on the pattern and stitch the light green highlights in the Borg cube. Then add the dark green (701) highlights.

4. Stitching from light to dark, and using the green highlights as reference points, fill in the shaded colors of the Borg cube: 414, 317, 413, and lastly black (310).

5. Trifold the fabric to hide the back of your stitches, and use a white thread to put five evenly spaced stitches across the back. This will ensure that it won't unfold later.

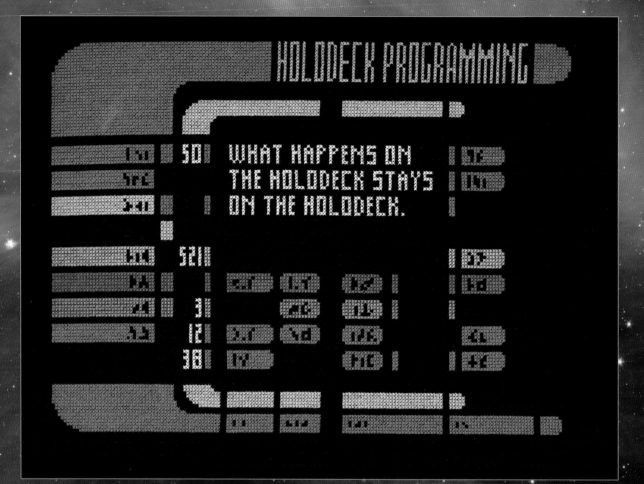

HOLODECK PROGRAMMING

WHAT HAPPENS ON
THE HOLODECK STAYS
ON THE HOLODECK.

"What's a knockout like you doing in a
computer-generated gin joint like this?"

–Commander Riker, "11001001"

what happens on the holodeck . . .

Pattern by Lord Libidan • **Stitched by Lord Libidan**

Everyone who watched *Star Trek: The Next Generation* wished they could have a chance to use the holodeck. The holographic projections of ski slopes, jazz clubs, and Sherlock Holmes mysteries grabbed our attention and helped us imagine what technology would be like in the future. If you had access to a holodeck, where would you go? I'd go aboard the *Enterprise* . . .

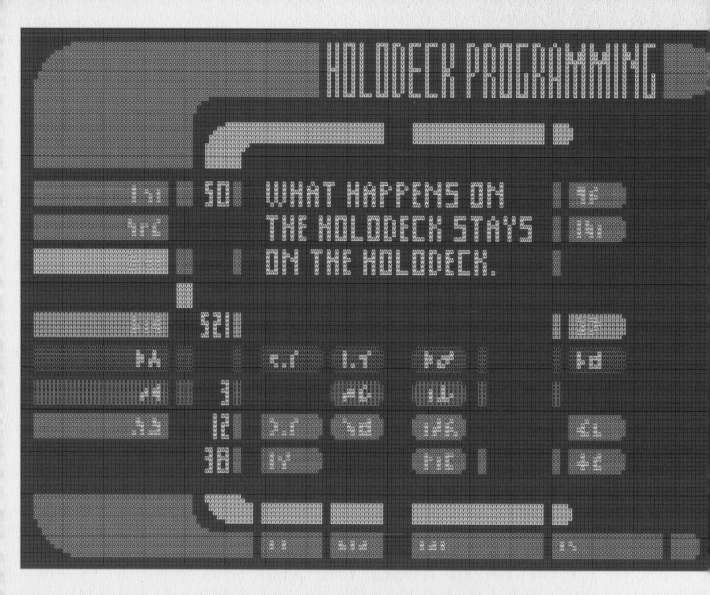

HOLODECK PROGRAMMING

WHAT HAPPENS ON
THE HOLODECK STAYS
ON THE HOLODECK.

 W — DMC 5200 Snow White
 T — DMC 210 Medium Lavender
O — DMC 740 Tangerine

M — DMC 3607 Plum
B — DMC 209 Dark Lavender
Y — DMC 725 Topaz

1. Cut your black aida fabric to a minimum area of 9.1" × 12.2". I recommend 12" × 15" so it will fit nicely into an 11" × 14" frame. Find and mark the center of the fabric.

2. Count up 6 and left 1 from the center to the H in HOLODECK and stitch the white (5200) of the text in the middle of the project. I recommend working in a counterclockwise circle through the text starting with the H.

3. Count down 12 from the center into the center dark pink (3607) bubble. Stitch to the right and left to finish out the pink row. Count up 2 from the dark pink row and stitch the light pink (210) row. Count down 2 from the dark pink row and stitch the purple (209) row.

4. In the lower right corner, count down 2 from the purple row and stitch the orange (740) row from right to left. Work up the left side and around to the upper right corner. To finish the very bottom row of orange, count down 15 from the second-to-last orange row and stitch from right to left.

5. Finish the colors by stitching the yellow (725) sections around the edges.

6. Finally, work around the outside of the project, filling in the random white letters and numbers. If the gaps between sections are more than about 6 stitches, I recommend tying off and starting the new area with a new thread.

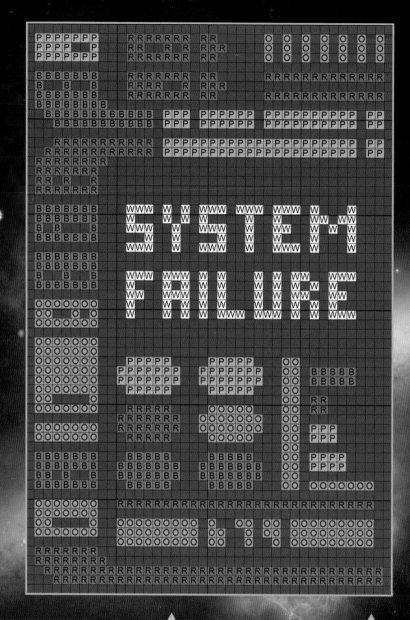

padd

Pattern by Lord Libidan

The Personal Access Display Device, aka PADD, is probably one of the only examples of our modern technology catching up to *Star Trek*. The idea of holding a flat, powerful computer in your hand seemed so far away when it first appeared on-screen, but now it has become part of our daily lives. This project would look great stitched onto a tablet computer sleeve.

 **instructions**

1. Cut your black aida fabric to a minimum area of 2.9" × 4.3". I recommend 5" × 7" so it will fit nicely into a 4" × 6" frame. Find and mark the center of the fabric.

2. Starting from the center in the letter I in FAILURE, stitch the white (5200) lettering in the middle of the project. Work in a counterclockwise circle, and don't bother tying off your thread.

3. Counting 12 down from the center, stitch the orange (740) by working down and around the bottom. Start a new thread and count 26 up and 7 right from the center to finish the orange at the top right.

4. Complete the lavender (210) by counting 7 down from the center and finishing the bottom section. Then start a new thread and count 16 up from the center and finish the top section.

5. Finish the project by completing the blue (799) and red (606) sections throughout the project. Tie off and start a new thread if the jump between sections is more than about 6 stitches.

"The needs of the many outweigh the needs of the few, or the one."

—*Spock, Star Trek II: The Wrath of Khan*

vulcan handkerchief

Pattern by Lord Libidan • **Stitched by John Lohman**

The Vulcan IDIC symbol (Infinite Diversity in Infinite Combinations) is the underlying principle behind Vulcan philosophy. The idea honors and pays tribute to the infinite amount of variation that can occur across the universe. This pattern mimics the IDIC pin that Spock wears with his dress uniform on occasion. Now you can blow your nose and admire the vast diversity of viruses and bacteria on your handkerchief.

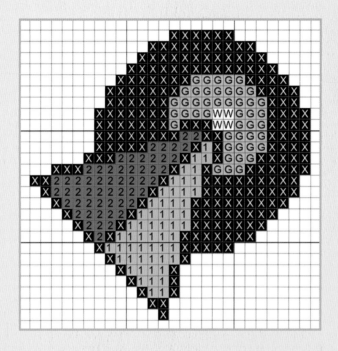

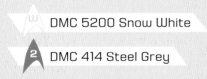 DMC 5200 Snow White

 DMC 414 Steel Grey

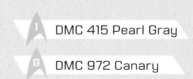 DMC 415 Pearl Gray

 DMC 972 Canary

 DMC 310 Black

1. To make your own handkerchief, take a 13" × 13" piece of square fabric and sew a ½" hem around the outside for a finished size of 12" × 12". A thin, white, all-cotton fabric is best for this project.

2. Cut a 3" × 3" square out of your waste aida canvas and stitch it onto the lower right corner of the handkerchief with a few baste stitches. These will be removed later, but they will keep everything aligned until you are finished cross-stitching. Mark the center of your waste fabric.

3. Start with the dark gray (414) at the center and stitch the upper gray triangle, working your way out from the center. It is very important that you work your way out from the center as it will smooth out the fabric. If you don't work out from the center, you could end up with bunched-up fabric in the middle.

4. Next, count 2 right from the center to stitch the light gray (415) of the bottom triangle. After the grays are done, stitch the gold (972) and white (5200) of the center circle.

5. Lastly, stitch the black (310) outlines, working from the center to the outside of the pattern in a counterclockwise circle.

6. Once the stitching is done, remove the baste stitches and wet the waste fabric. Waste fabric is held together by water-soluble glue and will fall apart into individual threads. Use tweezers to remove each waste fabric thread individually.

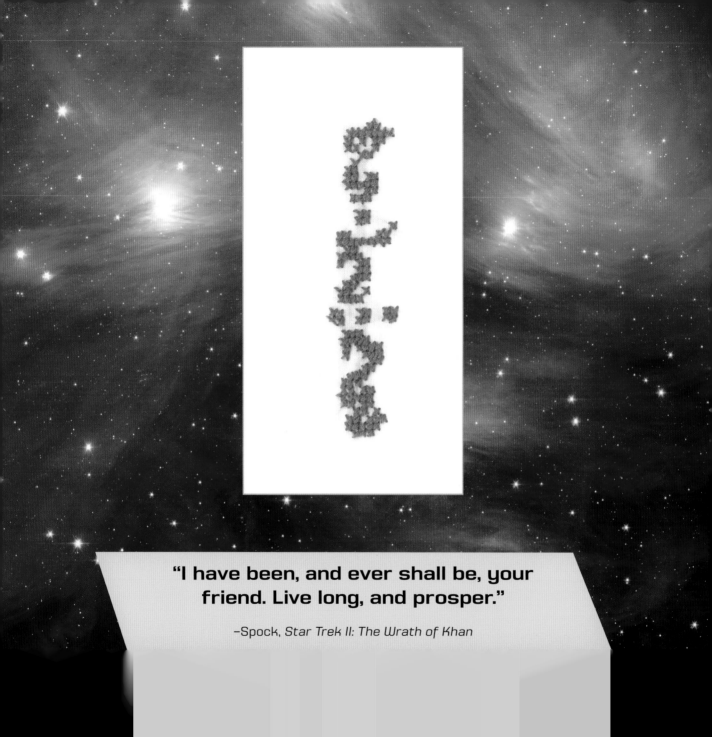

"I have been, and ever shall be, your friend. Live long, and prosper."

–Spock, *Star Trek II: The Wrath of Khan*

spock's burial robe handkerchief

Pattern by John Lohman

Stitched by John Lohman

I get goose bumps just thinking about Spock's death scene in *Star Trek II*. It will probably never be quite the same as the first time you saw it, when you actually thought Spock was gone for good. But at least now you can use your burial robe handkerchief to wipe your tears as you watch that final, heartbreaking scene.

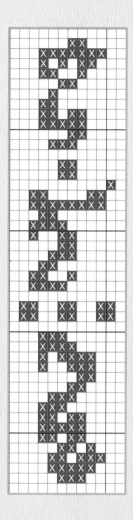

 DMC 3807 Cornflower Blue

1. To make your own handkerchief, take a 13" × 13" piece of square fabric and sew a ½" hem around the outside for a finished size of 12" × 12". A thin, white, all-cotton fabric is best for this project.

2. Cut a 2" × 4" rectangle out of your waste aida canvas and stitch it onto the lower right corner of the handkerchief with a few baste stitches. These will be removed later, but they will keep everything aligned until you are finished cross-stitching. Mark the center of your waste fabric.

3. It is very important that you work your way out from the center as it will smooth out the fabric. If you don't work out from the center, you could end up with bunched-up fabric in the middle.

4. From the center, start with the blue (3807) in the center symbol and stitch your way to the bottom of the pattern. Tie off at the bottom and start a new thread back in the center, working your way to the top of the pattern.

5. Once the stitching is done, remove the baste stitches and wet the waste fabric. Waste fabric is held together by water-soluble glue and will fall apart into individual threads. Use tweezers to remove each waste fabric thread individually.

Make it So!

"In your position, it's important to ask yourself one question: what would Picard do?"

–Commander Riker, "Pen Pals"

MAKE IT SO!

Pattern by John Lohman • Stitched by Emma Lenton

Here we have the classic catchphrase of the much-adored Captain Jean-Luc Picard—although he might have gone with "Make it sew!" if he'd ever gotten a taste of cross-stitch. I'm sure everyone has heard extended and emotional arguments about Kirk vs. Picard; the best way I've heard this argument ended is with the statement that Picard not only fenced with Whoopi Goldberg; he beat her.

DMC 5200 Snow White

✦ INSTRUCTIONS

1. Cut your black aida fabric to a minimum area of 9.4" × 10". I recommend 12" × 15" so it will fit nicely into an 11" × 14" frame. Find and mark the center of the fabric.

2. Count 4 to the left of the center into Picard's ear and start stitching the white (5200). I recommend working large areas in horizontal lines, doing half stitches all the way to the end of the row, then coming back on the same row to finish each X. Start a new thread any time you need to jump a large gap, such as the left side of his face.

3. Count 28 right and up 2 from the center into the I in IT. Finish the word and count up or down 11 from there to finish the MAKE and SO!. Make sure to start a new thread for each word so you don't leave large runs of white under the black fabric.

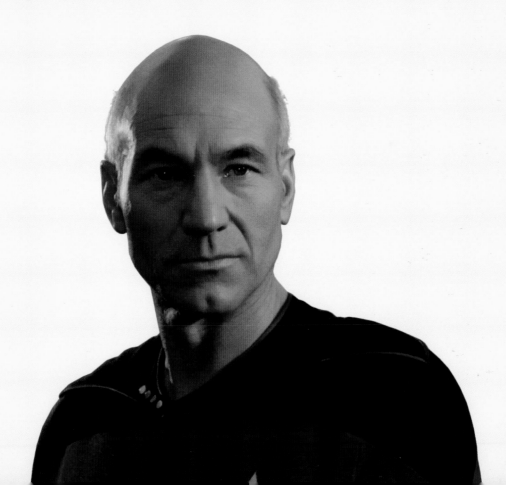

"My very first friend was a warp coil."

–Wesley Crusher, "The Game"

"shut up, wesley!"

Pattern by John Lohman • Stitched by Lindsay Bickford

Watching *TNG* wouldn't have been nearly as entertaining without young Wesley Crusher around to yell insults at. Never in history has a teenage boy been responsible for saving a whole starship from destruction while simultaneously annoying crew members and audiences alike. He wore many amazing futuristic (*ahem*: '80s) sweaters throughout the years, but he is shown here wearing the classic red, yellow, and green stripes.

 DMC 407 Desert Sand

 DMC 779 Cocoa

DMC 451 Shell Gray

 DMC 5200 Snow White

 DMC 898 Coffee Brown

DMC 310 Black

DMC 3779 Terra Cotta

 DMC 414 Steel Gray

DMC 902 Garnet

 DMC 840 Beige Brown

 DMC 3808 Turquoise

1. Cut your tan or gray aida fabric to a minimum area of 5.6" X 6.1". I recommend 9" X 11" so it will fit nicely into an 8" X 10" frame. Find and mark the center of the fabric.

2. Count up 5 from the center into the T in SHUT and stitch the white (5200) from the right side to the left to finish the word. Start a new thread and count right 15 and up 3 from the center into the U in UP. After you finish UP and the comma, count down 5 stitches and left 1 stitch from the tail of the comma into the ! and stitch through WESLEY! right to left.

3. Count 2 to the right from the center and stitch the large light pink (3779) section in the middle of Crusher's face, working in a counterclockwise direction.

4. Next, work out from the center of the face into progressively darker colors. I recommend going in the following order: 407, 840, 779, 898, and 310.

5. Next, do the gray (414) and silver (451) colors for the shading along the edge of the shirt.

6. Lastly, stitch the three colored stripes in Crusher's sweater, working down through red (902), yellow (840), and teal (3808).

"Assimilate this!"

−Worf, *Star Trek: First Contact*

borg cube ornament

Pattern by Lord Libidan

Stitched by Sherona Bauckham

The Borg are here and they will assimilate all the other ornaments on your tree. Don't be surprised when you find yourself under attack by assimilated snowmen, sleighs, and nutcrackers. I recommend also stitching the included *Enterprise* ornament (see page 127) so it can do battle with the Borg and keep your tree safe.

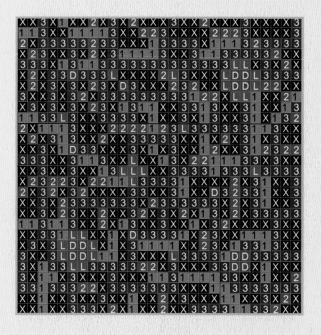

	DMC 413 Dark Pewter Gray		DMC 700 Christmas Green		DMC 310 Black
3	DMC 413 Dark Pewter Gray	**D**	DMC 700 Christmas Green	**H**	DMC 310 Black
2	DMC 317 Pewter Grey	**1**	DMC 414 Steel Gray	**L**	DMC 909 Emerald Green

INSTRUCTIONS

1. Cut six 2.5" × 2.5" squares of plastic canvas. You can find plastic canvas online or in the cross-stitch section of any major craft store. Find and mark the centers.

2. Stitch the pattern on each square from dark to light starting with black (310) and moving to dark gray (413), medium gray (317), and finally light gray (414).

3. Lastly, add the dark green (700) and light green (909) lights onto the Borg cube.

4. Cut the plastic canvas to shape around the stitched area. Don't cut into squares that contain any stitching.

5. Assemble the six squares into a flat cross and stitch the touching edges together using black (310). Make sure that you use a piece of thread long enough to stitch each edge in one piece. Start folding the edges into a cube and stitch the new edges as they come together. The last edge is the hardest, but it is doable if you start from the outside and stab diagonally through to the other edge.

6. Once you have your cube finished, add a loop of thread under a stitch in the center of the top square so that you can hang it.

"Fate protects fools, little children,
and ships named *Enterprise.*"

–Commander William T. Riker, "Contagion"

U.S.S. Enterprise tree ornament

Pattern by Lord Libidan • **Stitched by Justin Gourley**

As the star attraction for all of the series of *Star Trek*, the *Enterprise* will outshine even the star on your Christmas tree. This ornament pattern features the *TNG* version of the *Enterprise*, which has become so familiar to us over the years. I recommend starting a *Star Trek*-themed tree and adapting patterns throughout the book to cover your whole tree in geekiness!

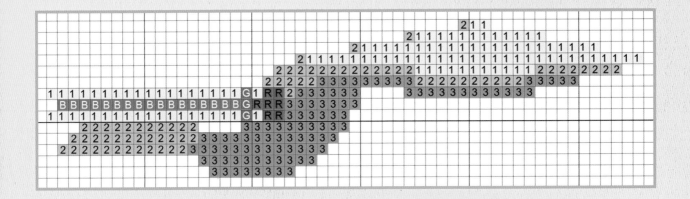

R DMC 606 Burnt Orange-Red

1 DMC 3072 Beaver Gray

B DMC 3843 Electric Blue

G DMC 3826 Golden Brown

3 DMC 318 Steel Grey

2 DMC 415 Pearl Gray

INSTRUCTIONS

1. Cut a 2" × 5" rectangle of plastic canvas. Find and mark the center.

2. Starting from the center, stitch the dark gray (318) of the bottom of the *Enterprise*. Try to stitch in horizontal lines as much as possible to keep the back looking neat.

3. Next, stitch the medium gray (415) in two parts, using a different thread for the bottom section and the saucer. To finish the main body, stitch the light gray (3072) in two pieces again: one for the engine and one for the upper saucer.

4. Stitch the blue (3843), gold (3826), and red (606) accents on the engine.

5. Cut the plastic canvas to shape around the stitched area. Don't cut into squares that contain any stitching.

6. Add a loop of thread to the top of the ornament so that you can hang it.

"One of the advantages of being a captain is being able to ask for advice without necessarily having to take it."

–Captain Kirk, "Dagger of the Mind"

WWCKD (WHAT WOULD CAPTAIN KIRK DO)?

Pattern by John Lohman • **Stitched by Jade A. Morton**

Captain Kirk often had his values tested with situations where none of his options were clearly ethical, yet he always seemed to make the right decision and land on his feet. Now, when you're faced with your own Earthbound struggles, all you have to do is look up at this beautiful framed artwork and ask yourself: What would Captain Kirk do?

 DMC 5200 Snow White    DMC 976 Golden Brown   DMC 310 Black

DMC 3856 Mahogany   DMC 433 Brown

1. Cut your black aida fabric to a minimum area of 10.7" × 6.9". I recommend 12" × 15" so it will fit nicely into an 11" × 14" frame. Find and mark the center of the fabric.

2. Starting with the white thread (5200), count down 7 stitches from the center to the first stitch in the middle piece of the first W. Finish the W to the left and then work your way through the rest of the letters to the right.

3. From the center, count up 2 and stitch the section of light brown (3856), working your way to the left. You need to tie off and start a new thread only if there is a large gap (about 6 stitches) between areas.

4. From the center, stitch the section of medium brown (976), working from the center out to the edges.

5. Finish the dark brown (433), and finally the black (310), using the same method of working from the center to the edges. The black stitches are optional because the aida fabric is already black—but it gives a more even texture if you do stitch it in. You also do not need to tie off any black sections, as the thread will be hidden behind the other colors.

A cross-stitch sampler showing the alphabet A–Z with the Star Trek phrases "Live long and prosper" and "To boldly go where no one has gone before"

"What does God need with a starship?"

–Captain Kirk, *Star Trek V: The Final Frontier*

traditional star fleet sampler

Pattern by John Lohman
Stitched by Erin KnightQuote

Cross-stitch samplers have been used for hundreds of years as a way to show off and test skills in needlework, and they commonly feature alphabets, quotes, animals, and decorative borders. We've adapted this traditional craft to the imagery of the future, including starships, planets, stars, and communicators. Crew members have downtime that needs to be filled, too, and I'm sure they would use crafting for relaxation just like we always have in the past.

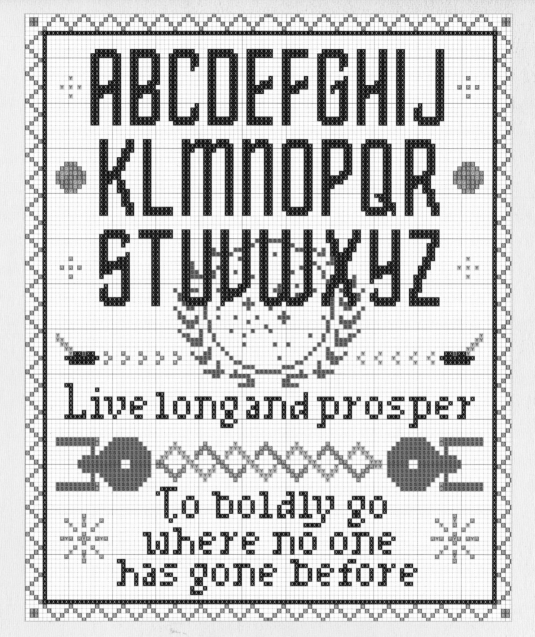

ABCDEFGHIJ
KLMNOPQR
STUVWXYZ

Live long and prosper

To boldly go
where no one
has gone before

B	DMC 798 Delft Blue	**R**	DMC 817 Coral Red
G	DMC 702 Kelly Green	**Y**	DMC 741 Tangerine

H DMC 310 Black

S DMC 414 Steel Gray

1. Cut your white aida fabric to a minimum area of 8" × 9.6". I recommend 10" × 12" so it will fit nicely into an 8" × 10" (or 8.5" × 11") frame. Find and mark the center of the fabric.

2. Count up 3 from the center into the bottom of the W in the alphabet to start stitching the black (310). The letters are close enough that you won't need to tie off in between them. Start a new thread and count 18 down from the center into the N in AND. Stitch to the left and start a new thread, working to the right to finish LIVE LONG AND PROSPER. At the end of the phrase in each direction, jump up and stitch the black parts of the communicators without starting a new thread.

3. Count down 17 from the N in AND into the L in BOLDLY and complete the bottom quote. To finish the black, count down 2 from the G in GONE and stitch around the outer black border.

4. Count down 2 from the center to stitch the gray (414) of the center symbol. Starting a new thread for each communicator, put the center gray dots in the communicators to the left and right. Lastly, count 5 down from the E in LIVE and the S in PROSPER to stitch the left and right *Enterprises*, working your way from the dish to the engines.

5. Stitch the red (817) and yellow (741) areas next. Make sure to start a new thread in each of the major areas to ensure that you don't have red and yellow threads showing up on the back of the white fabric.

6. Stitch the blue (798) border in a circle and make sure to jump into the two Earths as you pass by them. Stitch the green (702) land masses last, using a new thread for each planet.

'ej DoQ SoDtaH
ghoSpa' Sqral
bIQtIq

KLINGON SAMPLER

Pattern by John Lohman

It appears the Klingons have taken on a craft from Earth's past and made it their own. This Klingon sampler features the Klingon alphabet, *bird-of-prey* starships, ceremonial *bat'leth* sword, and warriors' *d'k tahg* knife. Cross-stitch might seem like a peaceful way to pass the time, but I bet the Klingons use *really* sharp needles.

INSTRUCTIONS

1. Cut your white aida fabric to a minimum area of 8" X 9.6". I recommend 10" X 12" so it will fit nicely into an 8"X 10" (or 8.5" X 11") frame. Find and mark the center of the fabric.

2. Start in the center, stitching the gray (169) of the central Klingon symbol, leaving a gap where the black alphabet overlaps the top spike. Start a new thread and stitch the gray in the weapons to either side. Stitch the brown (154) of the handles of the weapons; make sure to start a new thread for each weapon.

3. Starting with the unstitched gap that you left in the gray center symbol, stitch the black (310) of the Klingon alphabet. Work in a counterclockwise circle around the letters and make sure to stitch the black of the Qo'noS planets as you pass by them.

4. Starting a new thread, count 2 down from the bottom tip of the center symbol and stitch the black (310) Klingon quote at the bottom. Start new threads for the black in each weapon and starship, and the border.

5. Counting down 2 from the G in the bottom quote, stitch the dark green (3847) in the left *bird-of-prey* from top to bottom. Stitch the ship on the right. Finish the two planets, starting a new thread for each.

6. Finish the project by stitching the red (817) and yellow (741) details as well as the light green (702) border around the outside. Make sure to start a new thread for each section.

Aa Bb Cc Dd Ee
Ff Gg Hh Ii Jj Kk Ll
Mm Nn Oo Pp Qq
Rr Ss Tt Uu Vv Ww
Xx Yy Zz

AaBbCcDdEeFf
GgHhIiJjKkLl
MmNnOoPpQq
RrSsTtUuVv
WwXxYyZz

Alphabet Samplers

Pattern by John Lohman

There are so many memorable quotes throughout the *Star Trek* universe that we wanted to let you pick your own. With these two fonts, you will be able to take your all-time favorite quotes and design your own cross-stitch patterns. The first font is a traditional-style cross-stitch font, and the second one matches the font used in the credits from *TNG*. Cross-stitch software is great for setting up patterns and text. Another option is to use a piece of graph paper to plan out a design.

 DMC 310 Black

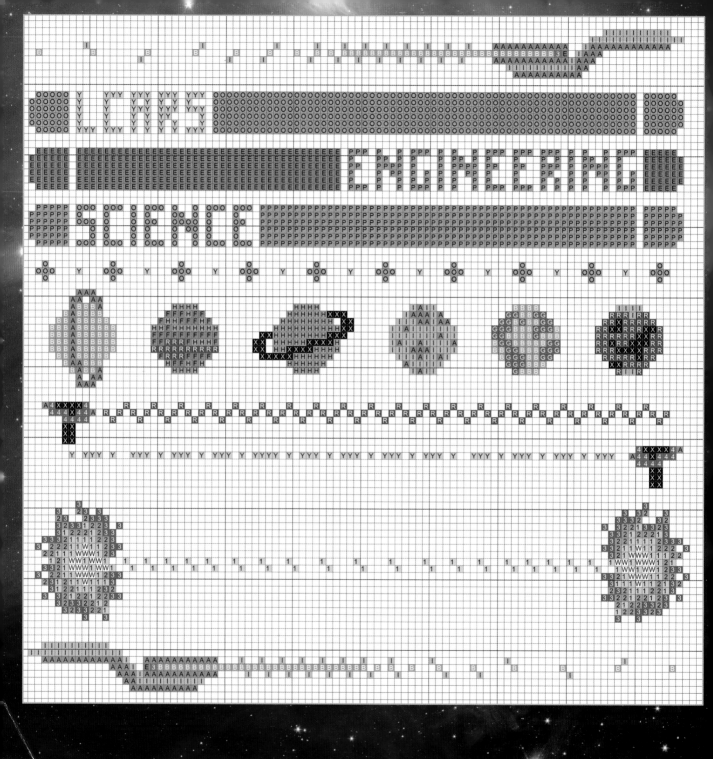

borders sampler

Pattern by John Lohman

Once you have chosen your favorite quote and mapped it out using the font patterns, you'll need a border to finish off the design. These border patterns include the *Enterprise*, wormholes, phasers, planets, and LCARS computer interface graphics. You can also choose any of the borders on other projects throughout the book. Choose your favorite border and start stitching! Once the text for your quote is set up, you can determine how large a pattern you will need. Use the above patterns as a guide to calculate how many times to repeat each motif to reach the edges of your text.

 DMC 5200 Snow White

 DMC 517 Wedgwood

 DMC 701 Christmas Green

 DMC 3761 Light Sky Blue

 DMC 794 Cornflower Blue

 DMC 742 Light Tangerine

 DMC 647 Medium Beaver Gray

 DMC 437 Tan

 DMC 931 Antique Blue

 DMC 996 Electric Blue

 DMC 3826 Golden Brown

 DMC 519 Sky Blue

 DMC 648 Light Beaver Gray

DMC 310 Black

DMC 221 Shell Pink

DMC 740 Tangerine

DMC 351 Coral

 DMC 3776 Mahogany

Acknowledgments

An extra special thank-you goes out to my international army of talented stitchers who made this book possible: Lord "Rhys Turton" Libidan, Lindsay "Yurtle" Bickford, Rosier "RMDC" Cade, China "Starrley" Darley, Callie "Celes_Lionheart" Beck, Jade A. "Jadely" Morton, Erin "Funkymonkey" Knight, Emma "Eveningemma" Lenton, Camilla "Petitcat" Schæffer, Carolyn "Carand88" Andolina, Sherona "Blackmageheart" Bauckham, Carrie "Blackberrybear" Musser, Alexandra "Ally" Pilling, Phillip "Philpepe" Coxwell, Amy Lohman, Katie "Katdun" Dunn, Megan N. "Kuja.girl" O'Donnell, Jennifer "Shanoa" Woodings, Deborah Dodson, and Justin "Doublej" Gourley.

A big thank-you to my editor, Kjersti Egerdahl, for getting me involved with this project. Thank you to Megan Sugiyama for designing the book, Kara Stokes for photo editing, and Jessica Eskelsen for taking the awesome photos.

A huge thank-you to my wife, Amy. Without her help while I neglected my household duties, this book would never have been finished on time. A future hello to my little ones, Molly and Foster; I can't wait until you guys are old enough to enjoy all of the nerdy pastimes that I want to pass on to you. And at last, a special thanks to my mom for getting me into crafting and my dad for getting me into *Star Trek* and science fiction at such a young age.

About the Author

John Lohman is a high school science teacher who resides in southern Oregon. He is the founder of the popular video game craft site and forums at Spritestitch.com. This is his first published craft book, and he has also contributed original works to *World of Geekcraft*, *Nintendo Power*, and *Craftzine.com*. John is an avid crafter, retro video game junkie, science fiction addict, and, most recently, a father of two.

Image Credits: